A beautiful soul.

To Love the Beast

Diana and Vincent's Story

J. Adams

Half man, half beast, Vincent is the recipient of unconditional love in his underground home–a Utopian society of outcasts living in a network of tunnels that were once part of an old subway system– yet he had never truly known the love of a woman. Walking through Central Park one night, he stumbled across a woman who had been brutally attacked and left for dead.

Breaking an underground rule and risking the exposure of the home of those who depended on him most, Vincent carried the woman there, and with the help of Father–the leader of the society below–nursed her back to health. He learned her name was Catherine. With her face being covered in bandages because of being slashed, she couldn't see the face of her caretaker. After the initial shock of Vincent's appearance, the two formed a bond stronger than love, and Vincent became not only her protector, but the love of her life.

Then, three years later, Catherine was kidnapped and killed after giving birth to Vincent's child, a beautiful and perfect son. Vincent was crushed by her loss and vowed to find her killer.

Diana Bennett, a detective for the police department, took the case, and together, they found the killer and Vincent was reunited with his infant son. A friendship formed between Vincent and Diana, and the people below welcomed her, entrusting her with the knowledge of their secret world, knowing she would never expose them.

Never allowing herself to be emotionally involved in a case, Diana's head told her what she felt for Vincent was nothing more than compassion for his loss.

But her heart felt something entirely different.

Catherine's death brought to Vincent a pain so great, he vowed to treasure his love for her forever, never allowing another in.

But that was before Diana.

This is their story.

For all my fellow Season 3 diehards!

"He is not to them what he is to me," I

thought: "he is not of their kind. I believe he is of

mine- I am sure he is- I feel akin to him- I

understand the language of his countenance and

movements: though rank and wealth sever us

widely, I have something in my brain and heart, in

my blood and nerves, that assimilates me mentally

to him."

— Charlotte Bronte, Jane Eyre

ne

New York City

Me

$\mathcal{T}$he tunnels are quiet, the distant tapping of the pipes fading with each step we take toward the gate leading out to Central Park. Vincent silently walks by my side, his gentle presence a boon of comfort, yet his nearness is emotionally unsettling. Having been privileged to attend the naming ceremony of his son–a child born of the love he shared with Catherine–my heart is full of gratitude for the blossoming friendship that has formed between us, a friendship that deems me worthy enough to have been there. It was a beautiful ceremony, made even more so by the tranquil moments I was able to spend with Vincent and hold little Jacob afterward. The motherless infant gazed up at me, cooing in response to my soft-spoken words. He is beautiful, and surprisingly, I could see not only Catherine in his perfect features, but a little of Vincent as well.

As we reach the gate, I pause a moment and look up at him. His profile is shadowed, but moonlight softly filters through the bars, falling on his golden mane, the shimmering strands framing his beautiful feline features. From the moment I found him lying in front of Catherine's grave, his unconventional beauty has not failed to stir feelings I keep buried in my heart.

"Thank you for allowing me to be a part of this special day."

His blue eyes meet mine. "My son is a gift, Diana. Thank you for reuniting us. I will never be able to repay your kindness."

"There is nothing to repay." I quietly gaze up at him another moment, my mind a jumble of thoughts, my head sifting through memories of the whole long ordeal. We faced more danger over the past months than either of us ever had before, but we made it through, and here we are. Anything could have happened–and it did–but God was smiling down upon us and the fates were kind.

Pondering this, part of our earlier conversation in Vincent's chamber comes back to me.

"Diana, you've done so much for us. Why?"

I take a moment to answer. "It's funny, I . . . when it was happening I never even questioned it. I don't know, Vincent. You make everything so possible, I couldn't help but want to help you."

"Jacob was not my only blessing."

"You're thinking of Catherine."

"Always . . . and I'm thinking of you." He raises his eyes to mine, causing my heart to pound like a drum.

"Sometimes I wonder how all of this can be happening . . . and whether I even belong here or not." I pause, searching for the right words. "Your world is . . ." The way he looks at me makes it hard to even form words. "I don't know where I'm going anymore. I don't know where I'll be tomorrow."

"Tomorrow will come, Diana. We can only live each day as it comes to us, with its pains and joys, and all of its gifts."

Drawing my thoughts back to the present, I smile, not really wanting to go back to my lonely life but knowing I must. "If you need anything . . ."

"I will come to you." Opening the gate, he inclines his head to me slightly and I do the same in return before exiting the tunnel and heading home.

Kneeling by the flower pot in my loft, I water the small rosebush, marveling anew at the brilliant booms grafted together. One is red, the other white. The bush had been Catherine's. I found it on her balcony and brought it home to nurture it, hoping to keep it alive. I gently finger the fragile buds.

Love and purity. Vincent and Catherine. The two pairs seem to be synonymous, inseparable. Part of me wonders if they will ever be separate. The other part wonders why I am even pondering it.

I think I'm tired. Making sure the apartment is secure–I'm a creature of habit–I turn off the lights and head to the bedroom. Stopping in the doorway, I run a hand down the wooden frame, taking in the repair work before turning on the lamp and scanning the room. Everything is just the way it was before bringing Vincent here. That night completely changed my life, and each and every moment–both terrifying and wondrous–will stay with me forever.

Two months ago.

After a lot of searching and acting on a hunch, I find Vincent lying beside Catherine's grave, cuts and burns covering his body. Out searching for her killer, he was caught in an explosion that took the life of a friend trying to help him, a man who also loved Catherine. I cover Vincent with his cloak and bribe a cemetery worker to help me get him to my car. I then take him up to my loft, tend his wounds as best I can, then lay him in my bed to heal. While he is unconscious, I sit next to him and study him; Holding his clawed hands in mine, I intermittently gaze at his face, taking in his marvelous lion-like features. Each time I leave the room, I return and repeat the process because he is so fascinating and beautiful.

I keep watch over him through the night, my mind immersed in the possibilities of his birth, his existence. A great and terrible beauty lay in my room. I am scared, disoriented and worried that he might not make it.

The night passes. Then he awakens and all hell breaks lose.

I run into the room to find him thrashing on the bed, clawing the mattress to shreds, knocking over the bedside lamp and destroying the table in the process. Then he goes still and sleep takes him once more. Grabbing my gun from the desk in the front room, I make a pot of coffee, pour a large mug-full, and settle myself in a chair across from the bed for another night, the gun lodged between my knees, pointed at him. I am so tired I can barely keep my eyes open, but I do my best to stay focused on him. Eventually losing the fight, I slowly drift to sleep.

Sometime in the middle of the night, Mark, a boyfriend my heart has never been completely committed to, stops by. I tell him he can't stay, words are exchanged, feelings are hurt, and he finally leaves. Being a criminal investigator, my work has always come first and he knew this. I usually give every bit of myself to the case I'm working on because it is the only way I don't lose focus. In some ways, maybe my work has always kept me from completely opening to him. He knew this too, which is why his hurt was far worse than mine. His feelings ran far deeper, and had we gone on, they probably always would. I watch his face disappear through the elevator window, a bout of sorrow sweeping through me for what could never have been. Closing the gate, I return to Vincent.

As I enter the room he again awakens. Lifting his head slightly, struggling to focus on me, he softly says, "Catherine."

"No," I reply, keeping my voice soft as well. "My name is Diana."

Exhaustion claims him. Closing his eyes, his head drops back to the mattress and he again sleeps. Moving back to the chair, I grab my gun and reposition for the night, and soon fall asleep.

A while later he reawakens, wild and disoriented. Staggering to his feet, he spins his massive body around a bit, and unable to get his bearings–and completely unaware of me backed against the wall–lashes out, splintering the bedroom door before collapsing on the floor. Heart pounding a mile a minute, I crouch in the corner, willing myself to calm down. Grabbing my gun, I take a seat once more, awake for the rest of the night, my thoughts running together. Nothing in my head is clear anymore.

He finally awakens again. My gun is aimed but hidden in the blanket draped over my shoulder. Sitting up and a little frantic, he backs against the wall, his eyes searching his surroundings before finally settling on me.

"Where am I?" His deep voice is a whisper, but still resonates around the room.

"In my loft . . . I found you in a graveyard behind St. Cleos."

"I don't remember." He tries to stand to leave but is unable and I slowly approach him.

"You brought me here?" He holds his head because it pains him to talk. I tell him he is hurt and has lost a lot of blood. I then assure him that he is safe and he rests his head on the floor, unable to move again. Taking the comforter from the bed, I cover him. Deciding there is no longer a need for my gun, I put it away, confident now that I'm in no danger.

Later when he awakens, I explain that I am investigating Catherine's death, vowing to do whatever I can to find the murderer.

And we did. My thoughts bounce back to the present. I couldn't have done it without Vincent. His courage and strength helped in more ways than I can count. Of course, no one will ever know what really happened–that I killed the crime lord responsible–shot him point blank, because prison would never have held him. I would do anything to keep Vincent and his son safe.

It has been a long day. Weariness finally setting in, I undress and climb into bed. As soon as I close my eyes, I dream.

Catherine's hair sparkles in the bright sun, her expression serene yet serious. She's beautiful, and sitting next to her on the park bench, I am overwhelmed by her warmth.

"Don't give up, Diana." Her voice is soft. "He needs you. You are a light in this sometimes dark world." Her eyes piercingly hold mine. "You are his *light."*

"Whose light?"

Smiling, she gets up and walks away, calling over her shoulder, "With time, hearts will come together and heal one another."

**wo**

One year later.

Vincent

eaning back against the pillows, Vincent closes the leather copy of *Great Expectations*, unable to concentrate. The dreams that have plagued him for the past few nights still burn in his mind, haunting his thoughts. He wishes he could talk with someone, share his night visions and ask for advice, but a great part of him is unwilling to face the visions forming in his head, so he struggles yet again to push them away, unable to deal with the feelings of betrayal.

Of his betrayal of another.

It has been three months since he last spoke with Diana, yet mere days since he last saw her. She is a strong woman, possessing one of the most amazing minds he has ever seen, and she can definitely take care of herself well enough. These are things he accepts and admires. Yet the sudden sense of protection he feels for her is something he is still trying to come to terms with.

Each week for the past year, he has gone to her street, stood outside her apartment building, and just gazed up at her loft, watching the light in her window. A couple of times he watched her where she stood on the rooftop, looking out into the night, and wondered where her thoughts strayed. Her determined innocence illuminated her surroundings, her conviction a light in the dark places of this world.

"She is your light, Vincent," is what Catherine had said at the end of this most recent dream–a dream that took place in another world, one where he and Diana shared feelings and acts that were familiar, yet completely new to him. It had only been a dream, but her touch still burns in his mind, the sensation of her fiery red hair and soft skin beneath his fingertips making the memory difficult to erase or let go. He repeatedly strives to convince himself that these thoughts are only those of gratitude for all she did for him and his son.

It is only that. Gratitude. The mental repetitive lie is losing its numbing effect, as is the war in his heart. *"Your light, Vincent."*

Is it any wonder sleep eludes him now?

Taking a deep breath, he runs a hand back through his hair. He senses no bond with Diana, at least not the kind he shared with Catherine . . . yet there is something that draws him to her. However, the mother of his child is still in his heart, his soul. He cannot allow himself to betray her. He cannot!

Placing the book on the bed at the sound of little Jacob's waking cry, Vincent lifts his son from his bed, holding him snugly in his arms. If any act holds Catherine close to his heart, this one does. Smiling contently, he again revels in his role of fatherhood, his gratitude for Catherine's love renewed.

Three

Me

"Got a file for you." District Attorney Joe Maxwell hands me a folder. "Neighbors reported this family went missing a couple of weeks ago. The father took the mother and twin girls hiking in the mountains and never came back."

"Maybe it was an extended vacation," I say, flipping through the file. There is a family photo, as well as single photos of each family member. The beautiful seven year old girls have blond hair and blue eyes just like their mother, and all three look fragile. The dark-haired father is handsome and owns an all-American look. They seem like your average family, completely normal. But I know from experience how deceiving looks can be.

"That's what the neighbors thought, but the family left their dog locked in the backyard with just enough food for a week. The neighbor kids have been checking on it and are taking care of it. This has never happened before, according to the wife. The husband said they were going up to Bear Mountain."

This is my job, but I hate it. Don't get me wrong, I love doing something so meaningful, but I hate certain aspects of it. In some cases I am successful, but many cases go unsolved or end tragically.

"Has forensics finished?"

"Yep, the place is clean."

"I'll get back to you."

"I figured you would."

Tucking the folder under my arm, I give Joe my usual mock two-fingered salute and he smirks. That's the kind of relationship we have–friends, but not close ones. While investigating Catherine's murder I got to know Joe a bit. He was emotionally involved in the case.

Because he loved her too.

But everyone loved you, didn't they, Cathy?

It seems connections to Catherine are all around me and I face them daily. All, that is, except the one I would gladly face if given the opportunity.

Vincent.

When I finally arrive home, there is a folded piece of paper sticking out of my mailbox.

Meet me above at nine. Please.

Heart skipping a beat, I unlock the door and head inside. Vincent wants me to meet him, and though gladness fills my heart, I hope everything is okay Below. I still have a half hour before he comes. Keeping my coat on and grabbing a book and a flashlight, I head up to the roof to wait.

"Diana."

I close the book, turning as he walks out of the shadows.

"Vincent." my breath catches.

His eyes travel to the book in my hands. "Jane Eyre."

"Have you read it?"

"Only once, long ago."

"It's one of my favorites."

"Perhaps I will read it again."

"You should."

He smiles slightly, then says, "Thank you for meeting me. I need your help."

"What can I do?"

He moves closer. "A little girl wandered into the tunnels. Pascal found her curled up in one of the narrower passages asleep. He carried her to Father."

"Did she say where she came from or how she ended up there?"

"She hasn't spoken. Father and Pascal have tried, but she hasn't said a word. She seems to be in shock, yet . . . somehow she knows me."

"What do you mean?"

"I was standing back in the corner wearing my cloak, trying to keep my distance. She saw me, ran to me, wrapped her arms around my waist and would not let go."

Strange. I mentally tick through ideas. "Is it possible that her parents were once tunnel dwellers and told her about you and the world Below?"

"It is possible, but how would the child know how to find us?"

I sigh. "I don't know, Vincent, but it's clear she has a connection to your world." I glance at my watch. "I know it's late, but can I see her?"

"I hoped you would come. She may be sleeping, but this is important enough to wake her."

"Okay . . . I'll meet you downstairs." Turning, I am the first to walk away, glancing back briefly. It still boggles my mind that he can scale buildings the way he does.

Nodding, he disappears into the shadows once more.

Four

We quietly creep into the children's chamber, quickly locating the bed where the child is sleeping. Somehow the people living down here have managed to take a large cavern and turn it into a cozy sleeping area for the children. There is a warm feeling here, one that exudes safety and security for all who rest their weary heads here. Not unlike Vincent's chambers, only there the warmth is different.

Squatting down, I gently move the blanket back from the girl's face while Vincent holds the lamp. Surprisingly, her features are as familiar as Vincent's because I've studied them so intently throughout today.

"Vincent, this child belongs to a missing family I started investigating today."

"Are you sure?"

"Yes. Her name is Jaimey Scott. Some neighbors reported them missing. They went camping a couple of weeks ago and haven't been seen since. I was still considering the possibility of an extended vacation, but now . . ." I softly touch the little girl's hand and her sleepy eyes open.

"Hi, Jaimey," I whisper. "How are you?" She stares back, wide-eyed. "Will you talk to me?"

She says nothing, but her haunted eyes hold much. They are the eyes of someone who has seen a lifetime of hurt. Rubbing her hand once more, I croon, "It's all right, honey. Sleep"

I follow Vincent out and we head to the library. Our walk through the dim stone corridors is silent, words being saved until we are there.

"She needs counseling, Father," I say to the older man sitting at the desk. "We have to get her to talk."

Father nods. "We have already contacted one of our helpers above. He is a child psychologist and will be here in the morning."

Vincent stands, moving next to me. "As I watched her sleeping, there was something familiar about her features, as though I have seen her before, but I haven't."

"Maybe you are remembering her mother."

"Perhaps, but the recollection escapes me."

Mentally exhausted, I rub the back of my neck. "Tomorrow I'm going to the family's home to get a feel for who they were." I heave an inward sigh, gearing myself up emotionally. This part is always hard, but it is also the only way I can work.

"Diana," Father says, standing, "let us know if we can help in any way."

"You already are, by keeping the child safe. That's what matters." I smile. "Thank you."

Vincent walks me back to the tunnel entrance.

"You are doing this alone?"

"Yes."

"There may be danger."

Turning, I look up at him, watching the breeze from outside play with his silky strands like fingers, making my own itch to touch his wild mane. "There is always the possibility, but not usually, at least not by this time in the case."

"Still, I worry for you, Diana."

His words warm me, so much so that I am about to say something I have never even considered when I'm working on a case. "Would . . . would you like to come with me?"

Vincent heaves a deep sigh. *Is that relief I hear?* "It would ease my mind greatly."

"The home is twenty minutes away, but Vincent, it will be daylight. I can wait until dark."

"No, that won't be necessary. I will find a way to meet you there."

"My car windows are tinted. No one would see you in the back."

Quietly pondering a moment, his eyes never leaving mine, he finally says, "I will come to you before dawn."

Five

*T*hough Vincent is near, he gives me space, allowing me to block his presence and focus. As usual, I slowly move through the home, internalizing my surroundings. The place has been remodeled, the smell of fresh paint and new carpet assaulting my nose. There are vaulted ceilings, chandeliers, leather furniture, and expensive tapestries throughout. And it's very clean, even the family room; all the dolls and other toys are placed neatly on shelves, the toy box meticulously organized. My mind reasons that Laura Scott wanted to leave their home clean before they left, but it seems like the family keeps a strict regimen and Jaimey and her sister Amy don't get to be as carefree as most children. Because of Roman Scott, maybe?

Was he the strict one? His photos do boast a commanding presence, someone who may like things a certain way. But then again, maybe my deductions are wrong. It's so hard to keep an open mind when it comes to children being harmed or going missing.

Each room I enter is the same: meticulous. Almost sterile. The closets, under the beds and bathroom and kitchen sinks. Everywhere.

"Too pristine," I murmur before heading out to the back yard. Vincent stands in the doorway, not wanting to risk unnecessary exposure. The yard is large, but I move around it quickly, ignoring the barking dog. Walking along the white picket fence, I stop at a spot that is loose with numerous scratches. Behind the fence is totally wooded. It looks like the dog has done the damage, but only in the one spot.

Why? I turn to the dog standing at the door of the run. *What were you trying to get to, boy?* Slowly approaching the German shepherd, I lift a hand to the gate, allowing the dog to sniff my scent. I feel Vincent's eyes on me, and I can sense his deep concern for my safety. The feeling is growing more familiar and is strong, sweeping through me, bringing me comfort. I know if the dog tries to attack me, Vincent will come to my aid.

"It's okay, boy. I'm trying to find your family. You want to help me?" Flipping the latch, I open the gate, a little startled when the dog races past me toward the same spot on the fence and starts scratching the wood. "What are you trying to get to?" Pulling hard on the loose board, I manage to pry it off, then another. The dog quickly squeezes through the opening and I duck through.

"Diana," Vincent calls and I turn. "What are you doing?"

"It's fine, I'll be right back." I run to catch up with the dog, wishing I knew his name to call out to him. Leaves crackle beneath my feet, filling the silent forest. The deeper into the woods I run, the more it dawns on me that the dog may just be after a rodent or stray cat that had been in the yard. That would be just my luck, to be led on a canine adventure. At another time it would be a humorous thought, but not now.

A a quarter of a mile later, I crest a hill and look down, spotting the dog several yards away sitting by a large rock, a low whine escaping his furry body. The closer I get to the animal, the harder my heart thumps. Then I see what is on the other side of the rock and my insides scream.

There lay the bloody remains of a child. The blond hair and size of the body are unmistakable.

Feeling faint, I sensed Vincent approach, and I turn, burying my face in his chest. His arms banding around my trembling body, he presses me into himself, holding me in silence. I'm grateful for that silence, because words of any kind would be wasted. Before coming today, I tried to prepare myself for the worst. I always do, and still hold on to the hope that the outcome will be good. But this . . . I never expected this–to come out today and find a child's battered body in the woods behind her own home.

Tightening my arms around Vincent's waist, my need for comfort–for *his* comfort–is filled by his muscular reciprocation, his warm breath in my hair where his face is buried. If I could stay wrapped up in him this way forever, I would, but reality draws me from his embrace.

"I need to take you back and then meet the police back here."

Vincent

Through the brave front, Vincent senses her pain, sadness, hurt, and anger. And he knows she needs him. She has always been a loner in life, having lost her parents years ago and seeing little of her sister. In life and in work she has been a loner for far too long, never needing anyone. Yet he senses her emotional need for him. And he is weary of fighting his feelings for her.

So tonight he will stop fighting, and give in to the longing plaguing them both.

"I will come to you tonight, Diana. Wait for me."

 Six

Me

Within an hour the entire neighborhood and the surrounding woods are crawling with policemen and agents. Since no one is willing to take the blame for not searching the wooded area more thoroughly, nothing is said beyond what is necessary to the case. The extended vacation scenario is completely off the table now and the search has been widened and now includes the surrounding states.

The sight that met my eyes earlier will never leave me, and as I reach my apartment building, I come to accept that we may never find Roman and Laura Scott or even know what happened. At the moment I can't think enough to contemplate it. I don't want to think anymore, period. Right now what I really want is something that will most likely never truly be mine.

I get out of the car and Vincent steps from the darkened doorway.

"Are you all right?" he asks me.

Swallowing against rising emotion, I answer honestly. "No."

Taking my hand, he leads me to the door, guiding me inside. This is the first time he has been in my apartment since that night. Exiting the elevator, I take off my coat and head to my workstation. Staring at the photo of Amy for a moment, I attempt to mentally shut down enough to unpin it from my board and put it back in the file. Closing my eyes, I rest my hand on the closed folder, feeling Vincent's hand cover mine only seconds later. I hadn't heard him move, he is just there. Then comes his deep voice.

"Diana." He large hands move to my arms, turning me to face him. "There is something I wish to –" The door buzzer cuts off his words and he moves away from me, grabbing his cloak.

"Don't leave. Please." I stare into his clear blue eyes, gesturing to my room, and he nods.

"Yeah?"

"Diana, it's Jacob."

Father? I push the button, unlocking the door. When he finally exits the elevator, Vincent comes from my bedroom.

"Father," he says, "what is it?" Since the old man rarely comes above, it must be important.

"I think I know who Jaimey's mother is."

"Would you like to sit?" I offer.

"No, thank you. When Vincent was just a boy, a girl was brought to the tunnels. She was nine and lived alone with her father who was abusing her. One of the neighbors happened to be a helper who knew what was happening, and she brought her to us. The father died a year later, drank himself to death. Oddly, he never reported the girl missing. An aunt came to take care of the burial. After talking with the woman, our helper came below for her. The child went with the aunt and we never saw her again. The woman's name was Lydia Stanton."

Walking over to the desk, I take a picture from the folder and show it to Father.

"Yes," he says. "I'm sure this is her. She was only a child then, but the eyes have the same haunted look."

"Do you have any idea where the aunt lives, or if she's even still alive?"

"None at all," Father answers.

"And the helper passed away a few years ago," Vincent adds.

I sigh. "Well, with the search expanded, hopefully a clue will turn up soon." *I pray one will, because I can't handle another sight like today..*

Sensing my thoughts–and don't ask me how–Vincent moves to my side, offering silent comfort.

After seeing Father out Vincent asks, "Will you be all right? Or would you like me to stay?"

"For a while. Please."

Wrapped in a blanket, we sit on the roof, our backs against the concrete wall, his arm around me. Even at this late hour, our surroundings are still buzzing with life. Of course, it *is* the city that never sleeps. The moon is full and lights up the sky like a Broadway neon sign.

"Tell me your favorite part of Jane Eyre," he says. His voice is a soft rumble against my temple.

I contemplate the novel a moment. "Well, I love the entire story, but truthfully, my favorite part is when Jane returned to what remained of the mansion after the fire and seeks out Mr. Rochester, who is now blind, having lost his sight in the fire." I smile, resting my head against his. "When she entered the room and he heard her voice, he thought he was losing his mind because he still loved her so. He had to hold her, to make sure she was real, because he'd thought she was lost to him. But now that she was there, he tried to push her away, thinking her love was spurred by pity and he didn't want to tie her to him, being only half the man he once was. All of it was far from the truth, and Jane was determined to prove to him that despite his disfigurement and loss of sight, he was worth loving, and he deserved happiness."

Smiling, I quote a couple of paragraphs..

"You touch me, sir,--you hold me, and fast enough: I am not cold like a corpse, nor vacant like air, am I?"

> *"My living darling! These are certainly her limbs, and these her features; but I cannot be so blest, after all my misery. It is a dream; such dreams as I have had at night when I have clasped her*

once more to my heart, as I do now; and kissed her, as thus—and felt that she loved me, and trusted that she would not leave me."

"Which I never will, sir, from this day."

"Never will, says the vision? But I always woke and found it an empty mockery; and I was desolate and abandoned--my life dark, lonely, hopeless--my soul athirst and forbidden to drink--my   heart famished and never to be fed. Gentle, soft dream, nestling in my arms now, you will fly, too, as your sisters have all fled before you: but kiss me before you go--embrace me, Jane."

"And then she kissed him. With no intention of leaving, of course."

Breathing in deeply, Vincent's embrace tightens. "I understand Rochester."

Drawing back a little, I look into his eyes. "I know. And I think he would understand you."

And believe it or not, I certainly know how Jane feels.

Before going to bed, I make a journal entry:

Today, the full extent of the brutality of man lay open before my eyes in the bludgeoned body of a child. I don't know if I'll ever truly be able to process it. Don't know if I

*want to. But I do understand a little better the ache of a
mother's loss. No, she wasn't my child, but the pain cut deep.
Still trying to hold onto hope for the mother (still not sure
about the father) but I don't know what to think. On to better
thoughts.*

*The feeling of sitting within the haven of Vincent's
arms tonight was one that will stay with me forever. If I died
tomorrow, I wouldn't forget.*

*I don't know how, but we have formed a connection I
never fathomed would exist between us. Not sure if it's real,
but it is enough. For now.*

eyen

One week later.

Me

"Come in, Diana."

Joe closes his office door and I take a seat across from him. Judging by his expression, whatever he has to tell me can't be good.

"We just got the call. A van registered to Roman Scott was found in a wooded area just outside of Jersey. Two bodies were inside, the victims bludgeoned to death. It's them."

Closing my eyes, I lean back in the chair, my face raised to the ceiling. *The husband was innocent after all.* "How long have they been dead?"

"Nothing conclusive yet, but forensics is thinking just a few days." He heaves a frustrated sigh, matching my feelings perfectly. "The two areas where the victims were found are so random, there's no telling where or even if we will find the other daughter."

Schooling my features, my mind goes over it all.

They are missing for two weeks. One girl turns up in the tunnels, alive. The other suffers a violent death in the woods behind her home. The parents are found murdered outside the state. What are we missing?

"Camping gear?" I ask.

"It was all there. Looks like it was recently used."

So they finished camping and were probably ready to head home. They loaded their gear and left the site. But . . . how did Jaimey make it back alive? She couldn't have unless . . .

The killer let her go.

"I need to get back into the family's home."

"Why? The place is clean."

My eyes pierce his. "Maybe I missed something."

"Okay." He knows my look by now. "Take another look."

It is noon when I enter the Scott home. Even after NYPD traipsed through the house again, everything is still pristine, not even a speck of dirt spotting the floor. I again make my way through each room, looking for something–anything that can give me some sort of mental direction, maybe give me a hint of a motive for the killer's actions.

I enter the kitchen again, opening and closing cupboards, going through drawers, looking for something I might have missed before. Then I hear a sound coming from another room.

Reflexes instantly kicking in, I pull out my gun and slowly exit the kitchen, checking both ways as I ease down the hallway. I am just entering the living room when something hard lands against the back of my head and I fall. Turning over, my vision is slightly blurred, but I just make out the feminine features of my attacker before I am hit again (she isn't alone) and my world goes dark.

I awaken in a dimly lit room, my hands and feet tied together, my body chained to some screws in the concrete wall. Eyes adjusting, I scan my surroundings. I'm in the unfinished part of the basement. I'm not sure of the time or how long I have been here , but the darkening sky is visible through the small window high above the washer and dryer. I was supposed to meet Vincent Below at six and he is probably wondering where I am.

At the sound of the door opening, I look up and watch the well-tanned, stylishly dressed blond descend the stairs.

"Ah, you're awake. I was afraid I'd killed you." She smiles, exposing straight white teeth. "And we can't have that. At least, not yet."

Onto her obvious baiting, I choose to remain quiet and let her do the talking. I am used to keeping a cool head and have become good at it. It has always paid off. Hopefully, it will again tonight.

"Diana Bennett. You're probably wondering how I know you and why you are here. Well, to answer to first question, I *don't* know you. We've never met. But I do know who you are."

Okay, who am I?

"You are the person that destroyed my life and took everything from me."

How did I do that and what did I take?

"You took from me the only man I have ever loved. Gabriel."

Ah. Remaining expressionless and keeping my voice even, I reply, "Gabriel killed a woman and kidnapped her child."

"What Gabriel did is of no concern to me. He was a good man and didn't deserve to die, especially not by your hand."

"How do you know it was me?"

She snorts. "Please. I have many reliable eyes, and one pair was still there that night when you assumed all of Gabriel's lackeys had left the mansion and you were alone." She reaches into her pocket, producing a gun, which wasn't unexpected. "He heard your final words to Gabriel before pulling the trigger. *"This was Catherine Chandler's gun,"* you said before shooting him straight through the heart."

Revenge? All of this because– "What did the Scott family have to do with this?"

"Absolutely nothing. They were just a tool to get to you, a very unlucky one. Of course, they were easy to use, especially since I was sleeping with the husband."

So he wasn't innocent after all. "You were having an affair with Roman Scott?"

"For a couple of months, actually, but love has a tendency to be one-sided in these situations. However, it was a strong obsession on his part. Strong enough to abandon his family on their vacation and meet me. So I took care of them. Then him."

Definitely a narcissistic attitude.

"Gabriel said your mind was brilliant but wasted at the police department. I knew that as soon as the family was reported missing, District Attorney Joe Maxwell would put you on the case. And the grizzly death of one child near her own home was sure to seal the deal. It was so predictable, just like Moreno agreeing to be one of Gabriel's front men. Gabriel owned every man he came in contact with that held a powerful position, and they were all at his beck and call." When I arch a brow, she smiles. "Oh, yes, I knew all about his ties to Moreno and the DA's office before the man's demise. I knew many things."

Keep her talking, Bennett. Keep her talking. "Why did you let one child go?"

"Just a small act of kindness to keep the case open and give you a bone to chomp on. Plus, I figured that in a sense, it would give the parents a little peace of mind." She crosses her arms, exposing some cleavage at the top of her tailored white blouse. "Poor thing was pretty shaken up when I released her. Did she say anything to help?" The question is asked with a quirked smile, like she obviously already knows the answer. "Tsk, tsk, at least she made it back."

Now that I have answers, this game is getting old. "So, now what?"

"Tired of playing already? Well, I'll only keep you a few minutes longer, and I'll even spare you a gruesome death and be merciful. After all, you were merciful to Gabriel, right?"

${\mathcal{E}}ight$

Vincent

${\mathcal{D}}$iana is late, and she is never late.

Racing through the tunnels, Vincent tries to calm his heart, drawing on a safer emotion– anger. He hasn't experienced such an emotional surge of anguish since before Catherine died. And that he has formed such a bond with Diana is both awe-inspiring and terrifying. He can't go through another loss. He can't bear *her* loss, because it would surely be the death of him this time.

Why have I waited so long to share my feelings with her? Growling, he struggles to shake away the desperate thoughts filling his mind. *She is all right. She has to be.*

Hold on, Diana. Please, just hold on.

Me

My face stings from the double slap against my cheek.

And now I am afraid, because I can see no way out of this. I have been in this situation before, when I was captured by Gabriel's men and brought to him, only I wasn't bound with a gun pointing at me. He'd had a motive for letting me live. Showing me Vincent's child and claiming the infant as his own son had all been part of the plan. Gabriel wanted me to tell Vincent because he knew Vincent would come for his child.

No, this woman is driven by something entirely different: pure unadulterated revenge. And because I know how much of a loner the self-exiled man was, I don't really believe the woman's love was reciprocated, but I am not about to say this now. What purpose would it serve?

"I hope you have loved ones, Diana, because now it is their turn to experience the kind of pain I did."

She moves closer, raising the gun to my head, and my only thought is of Vincent and my missed opportunities with him, of how much I love him. But as I close my eyes to await the quick jolting pain before death takes me, a man's death cry echos and a roar fills the basement as Vincent knocks the door off its hinges. Leaping over the steps, he dives toward my captor. Gasping, she turns the gun on Vincent, but he knocks it from her hand and sends a massive clawed hand across her face, ripping skin away and snapping her neck instantly.

Releasing a raspy breath, my eyes meet Vincent's and he comes to me and breaks my imprisoning bands. I am immediately swept up in his arms, crushed against his chest, his voice murmuring into my hair over and over, "I can never lose you, Diana. I will always keep you safe."

Agreeing to meet Vincent back at the loft, I straighten my appearance, put the chains and bindings in the trunk of my car, and call Joe to tell him what I've found: two bodies, one upstairs and the other in the basement, both of them suffering an unexplainable death, possibly an animal attack. Or maybe they were the victims of a copycat killer from a year ago, if not the vanished 'slasher.'

Just like in the past, the police department will probably never know.

Nine

Me

Standing with my head pressed against the shower

wall, I let the hot water run over me, trying to wash away the sadness and other foreign emotions of this day. I had been closer to death than ever before and was sure I would never see another day. But then Vincent came. He sensed me in danger. He actually sensed where to find me! I am still blown away by the strength of his empathic abilities. Of mine! Abilities I never thought I would ever possess. He knew I needed him and he was there. He killed for me.

"I can never lose you, Diana," he had said. *"I will always keep you safe."* Closing my eyes, I struggle to swallow back a day's worth of emotion, but it continues to

press and I can no longer fight it. Shoulders trembling, I let the tears come, giving thanks to God that I am still here, that I still have more life to live.

Exiting the bathroom, I find Vincent standing in my work area, staring at the empty board. He has taken off his cloak, his stitched shirt made in the world Below open at the collar, exposing a small patch of a massive chest covered in spun gold. As my eyes travel over him, sudden heat and longing fill my insides.

"Hey," I say, my breath raspy, and he turns. "Where are you."

Giving me a slight smile, he approaches me and fingers a lock of my damp hair before taking my hands in his. "Here, just thinking."

"About?"

He doesn't answer me right away, just simply stares. Closing his eyes, he drops my hands and delicately catches my face between his palms, moving closer. My breath hitches, my heart threatening to pound through my chest. I can't breathe and I can barely think because his actions have caught me so off guard.

"I want . . . I need . . ." His lips touch my forehead and all thought leaves me. Slowly, they travel to my cheek and then the other before making a warm path to the corner of my mouth. Releasing a shaky breath, my lips part. Then his warm mouth claims mine and timidness gives way to intensity as tongues and hands intimately explore. From the first moment I imagined him kissing me months ago, I wondered what he would tastes like, but never could my imaginings have ever done justice to the reality of it. His scent, his taste . . . it's every amazing thing I've ever imagined in my life and more.

"Diana," he groans and I answer with an emotional moan. Lightly running my tongue against the cleft in his lip, the groan increases, his embrace tightening. "Diana," he repeats, drawing back enough to look into my eyes. "I . . . my heart overflows with love for you, and in your arms is where my happiness lies."

"Vincent," I breathe, afraid to believe what I'm hearing. "You really love me?"

"I didn't think my heart would ever open again, but it has. "I truly love you. You are in my soul and I ache for you."

"I love you, too, Vincent." Pausing, I swallow hard. "I was afraid to allow myself to because I didn't think there would ever be room for me."

Brushing his lips against my brow, he whispers, "There is room for only you. Don't be afraid, for all that I am is yours." Trailing is lips back to mine, we kiss, devouring one another until we are breathless.

"I have thirsted for you, Diana, but like Jane Eyre's Rochester, I couldn't believe your vision of me could be unconditional, that you could truly desire me, no matter how much I wanted it to be so. Not that I thought you shallow. I just . . ."

"You just?" He doesn't continue and I press again, "You just what, Vincent?"

Releasing me, he turns away and puts space between us, but I have no intention of letting it stay. Moving to him, I take his hands. "Tell me, Vincent. You can say anything to me. You know that."

He finally raises his eyes to mine, his countenance solemn. " Diana . . . I need far more from you than I can offer, with only a commitment of my love and all that I am as trade."

Breathlessly, I squeeze his hands, the timid, proud and intense violence of his emotions rolling through me, residing *in* me. I know what is in his heart, and the sacrifices that would be required on my part. And casting my eyes around the loft that has been my home for so many years, I realize instantly that I would give everything and consider it no sacrifice, but a blessing to do so.

"Ask me, Vincent. Your love and all that you are everything I could ever want, and I offer you the same." I press his knuckles against my lips, my cheek. "Ask me. What do you need from me?"

Taking a deep breath, he says with conviction, "Marriage. I need *you*, Diana. Will you be my wife, live and share my life Below, and be Jacob's mother?"

As the first tear trails down my face, he gently brushes it away. "Yes, Vincent. I will be your wife and live with you Below. And as much as I adore Jacob already, it will be an honor to be his mother."

Taking my face in his hands, he closes his eyes and rests his forehead against mine. "You truly are a gift to me, one that I will cherish far beyond my last breath on this earth."

"And you will always be a part of me, Vincent. Always."

"Always," he echoes.

Vincent

A warm shudder rolls through Vincent as he is again immersed in her softness, his fingers buried in silky locks of crimson. He'd felt her emotions in the shower, and when she exited and came to him . . . oh, heavens, he'd felt them then, too! The longing, the aching need that flowed through their newly strengthened bond only served to feed his.

He passes the hours sitting on the sofa with Diana cradled in his lap, her beautiful face buried against his neck, his arms securely enfolding her. For a moment, the dream that plagued him for so many nights briefly claims his vision.

He and Diana are sitting on a deserted beach. The sun has faded in the distant horizon and the moon soon fills the sky, it's light shining down on them where they lay on a blanket holding one another. No words are spoken, but passion spills freely between them as they drink of each other deeply. But one primal phrase flows from his mind to hers through their bond before that same passion drives them to become one.

"You are mine, Diana. You are mine. You are mine . . ."

Drawing his thoughts forward, his embrace tightens for a moment. "You really are mine," he murmurs. Standing, he carries her to the bedroom and places her beneath the covers, kissing her sleepy head before heading back to the tunnels and his lonely chambers, taking comfort in the knowledge that they won't be lonely for much longer. Nor will his bed or sleep be solitary. For Diana will be his wife, his mate, his lover, and the keeper of his heart.

en

Me

"Joe, I need to talk to you," I say, entering his office.

"Okay, I've got a minute. Have a seat."

He is wearing his baby blue shirt and dark paisley tie, which can only mean one thing. "Taking off early with Jenny?"

He smirks. "How did you guess, detective?"

"Just a hunch."

"You know, you're too observant for your own good sometimes."

"That's what you pay me for." I smile at the goofy grin that always explodes across his face when his new favorite subject comes up. Jenny was Catherine's best friend and Jenny and Joe grew close as they grieved over their mutual loss. As much time as Joe spends with Jenny on his off time, it's safe to say their relationship has notched up another level.

How you do bring people together, Cathy.

"So talk to me , Diana." His prompt helps me rein in my thoughts.

"I've decided to go off the grid for a while."

He sits back in his chair. "How much time do you need?"

Sighing, I place my badge on the desk and watch his eyes widen. "This is indefinite."

"Now, hold on. I know this last case was hard on you, so take some time off, but don't quit, Diana. We need you. And we're not closing the case yet. There is still another little girl out there. I know the chances of finding her alive are slim, but she still needs to be found."

"I know. But if she *is* dead, she's safer now, isn't she?" I rub my temples, wishing that I could share Jaimey's location but knowing I can't. "I'm sorry, Joe, put someone else on it. This is something I've got to do. I'll keep in touch."

Joe's look is resigned. He knows me well enough to know that when I've made a decision, nothing will change it. "Are you sure?"

"I'm sure."

"All right," he sighs, standing and I stand as well. "But when you're ready to come back, your job is still here."

I nod and he reaches out to shake my hand, but we hug instead.

"Take care of yourself."

"You, too, Joe."

I exit the office, waving at Jenny where she sits waiting for Joe. She waves back, a wide smile on her face when she sees him behind me. I'm sure it won't be long before I get word of an announcement. They deserve their happiness. We all do.

"You were right, Cathy. With time, hearts can heal one another, and they have."

A sense of humility, awe, happiness, and closure fills me as I stand before Catherine's grave.

"It seems like years since I was here. Then again it seems like only yesterday. The night I watched Vincent fall to your grave altered everything. I had searched so hard for him, trying to put the pieces together and solve your murder. Then I turned his unconscious body over and gazed at his face, and I was changed, every concrete thing I ever believed vaporized, faded into nothingness." Pausing, I gaze out over the cemetery. "You had no idea how your death would affect my life, or his. But you fixed it, didn't you? Vincent shared his dreams of you with me and I did the same. And you knew. Somehow you knew we needed each other. I thank you for that."

Folding my arms against the chill, I take one last look at the rose I placed on her headstone when I first arrived. "Thank you," I whisper once more before walking away, leaving one life behind for a new one, a life that I am sure will give new meaning to my old one, and be my very reason for existing on this earth.

Epilogue

"Even the greatest darkness is nothing, so long as we share the light."

It is Winterfest! And our wedding day.

Standing in the great hall, surrounded by my new tunnel family, Vincent and I pledge our undying love to each other. Rings are exchanged, Father pronounces us husband and wife, and my life is complete. There is only a chaste kiss, our preference to indulge in a more passionate sharing away from numerous eyes mutually understood. But the happiness radiating from us is unmistakable.

Since the traditional opening of Winterfest was done before the wedding, we mingle for a bit, accepting well wishes before joining Father at the main table. The day is filled with good food, conversation, games and entertainment, and much laughter. And I even experience another first: making friends with a raccoon! Mouse, one of the young tunnel dwellers, managed to sneak his pet into the great hall and insisted I meet him.

We receive many gifts, but the one I will treasure most is Jaimey's. Her beautiful charcoal drawing of the two of us leaves us all amazed at her talent. Though she still hasn't spoken, the psychologist helper works with her regularly and thinks she will eventually be okay.

The love and acceptance I have received since meeting Vincent has increased tenfold on this day, causing a familial warmth to radiate over my whole being. And when we finally say goodbye and leave the festivities, I realize that I truly have a family now, one of my very own.

I am indeed blessed.

Having left Jacob in good hands for the night, Vincent leads me to a secluded cavern where there is a clear warm lake. In a far corner next to the wall sits a large palette covered in silky white sheets and a thick quilt. Beside it is a table bearing fruit and a bottle of red wine. Vincent moves behind me.

"It's beautiful," I say, hoping I don't sound as nervous as I feel. Having been with a man before, I am not afraid, just a little anxious about delving into the unknown. "Thank you."

His lips softly brush the back of my neck, slowly traveling to the side, and my eyes slip shut at the sensation, my heart quickening. His hands move around my waist and I turn, meeting his lips with mine, his warm mouth coaxing and setting me on fire with intoxicating voracity. Wrapping my arms around his neck, he lifts me, carrying me to the bed, and I am soon lost in the heavenly bliss of his love, never expecting the rapture that my body experiences from his, or the heat that fills me at the touch of his hands, his mouth. He is all man, with the physique of a Greek god, owning the heart of a man consumed with love, exhibiting the ferocity of a being claiming his mate, and the gentleness of someone possessing something so fragile that care flows from his every touch.

Tonight is everything, and much more.

Later on as I lay in Vincent's arms, I contemplate our unknowingly parallel lives and the events that brought us together. And all I can do is repeat the same thing again and again: *Thank you, Catherine, for bringing me to him.*

"Don't ever leave me," comes his raspy voice in my ear. His breath is sweet and warm, the familiar tone rumbling through his body to mine.

Rising slightly, I press a hand against his cheek, gazing into his beautiful eyes. "In the words of our dear Jane, with my own embellishment, of course, "I will be your neighbor, your nurse, your housekeeper, your friend and lover. When you are lonely, I will be your companion--to read to you, to walk with you, to sit with you, to wait on you, to be eyes and hands in those places you cannot tread. Cease to look so melancholy, my dear master and husband; you shall not be left desolate, so long as I live."

"Diana," he murmurs, pulling me down to him.

"Vincent," I whisper against his ear, nuzzling his hair, "if ever I did a good deed in my life--if ever I thought a good thought--if ever I prayed a sincere and blameless prayer--if ever I wished a righteous wish,--I am rewarded now. To be your wife is, for me, to be as happy as I can be on earth.""

About the Author

J. Adams is the author of interracial, young adult and inspirational romance, as well as romantic fantasy. She is a wife, mother of eight, and a grandmother. Armed with a library of her favorite books and a healthy stash of orange Tic Tacs, she and her family reside in Utah.

Jewel loves hearing from her fans, contact her at
jewela40@gmail.com
To check out Jewel's other books, visit her website at
JewelAdams.com
And stop by her blog: **jewelsbestgems.blogspot.com**

Other books by J. Adams/Jewel Adams

The Wishing Hour series

The Legacy series

Tears of Heaven

The Journey series

Against the Odds series

Mercedes' Mountain

Sweet 21 Birthday Ball

Say What You Need to Say

New

Stories of the Heart Christmas Short Story Collection

Forbidden Portals: The Quicksilver Project

Letters In the Moonlight of Taj Mahal - ebook

Like the Wind - ebook

For Love of Angel - ebook

The Passionate Hearts Novelette Collection - ebooks